MURDER MAKES A TOAST

Rooftop Garden Cozy Mysteries, Book 10

THEA CAMBERT

Summer Prescott Books Publishing

CHAPTER 1

As newlywed Alice Maguire-Evans stood on the balcony of the inn where she and her husband, Luke, were honeymooning, she thought she might actually be in heaven. A warm spring breeze blew her red curls out of her face and she sighed, deeply contented. The view through the huge trees that surrounded the gracious old inn was of the yard, which was scattered with tucked-away park benches, small tables and chairs, and mini gardens featuring blooms in every color. The lake lay over to the right, robed in the glistening hues of the sunset. The huge, organic garden that supplied the kitchen with fresh produce lay to the left, and past it were the orchards, showing the first tender apple blossoms of the season. And beyond all of that, in every direction, were rows upon rows of grapevines. A couple hundred acres of them. It was as though this magical spot, surrounded by the ancient Smoky Mountains, had been one of God's own favorite places, and Alice felt she could stay here forever.

It had only been two days since she and Luke had arrived at the Emmerson Estate Farm and Vineyard, which lay just outside of Little Bavaria, Tennessee, but those two days had been sheer bliss.

Alice turned and smiled at her husband, who was seated in a chair nearby, reading. "Can you believe this place is only two hours from home and neither of us had ever heard of it?"

"It's got to be one of the best kept secrets in the state," said Luke, closing his book and joining Alice at the balcony railing. He took her hand and kissed it. "I'm glad we made the time to get away."

The two had gotten married just before Christmas, and it had taken them until late April to come on this honeymoon. They'd meant to do it sooner, but there were the holidays to celebrate first, and then there was time spent moving Alice into Luke's lakeside cabin in Blue Valley, where Alice owned a bookshop on Main Street called The Paper Owl, and Luke was the head—and only—detective on the Blue Valley police force.

Now that they were married, they'd be splitting their time between the cozy apartment above The Paper Owl, and the peaceful cabin on the lake, which were only about ten minutes apart. The two locations were equally charming in their own ways. The bookshop apartment was perfect for weekends and festival days, and its French doors opened out onto an amazing rooftop garden that overlooked Main Street.

They shared the garden with the other inhabitants of the building—who also happened to be Alice's dearest friends. Owen James, who owned the bakery, Sourdough, lived on one side, and Franny Brown-Maguire, who owned the coffee shop, Joe's, lived on the other. Fate had been especially kind to the three friends through the years, because now, they were *also* neighbors out on the lake.

Franny had married Alice's older brother, Ben, just under two years ago, and the previous summer, they'd welcomed baby Theo into the world. Ben had lived in the little house next door to Luke's cabin for years, so now Franny lived there too. Then last fall, Owen had moved to the lake as well, into a charming old cottage just around the shore from Luke and Alice, which he'd lovingly renovated. As it stood, the group of friends were neighbors both on Main Street and at the lake, and that suited them all just fine.

"I wish Franny and Ben and Owen could see this place," said Alice. "Someday maybe we can all come back here together."

"That'd be great," said Luke. "I mean, we never would have found this place if it weren't for Owen."

Owen, who was the biggest romantic fool of the bunch, had written down the story of Alice and Luke's meeting and subsequent love affair and had entered it in *Fabulous Bride Magazine*'s Dream Honeymoon contest—and had won. As a result, Alice and Luke's weeklong stay at the luxurious Emmerson Estate Farm and Vineyard was an all-expenses paid extravaganza that included fun activities every day. The only catch was that Alice and Luke had been required to agree to attend each and every fun activity and have their picture snapped for an upcoming

Fabulous Bride Magazine spread—a small price to pay, in their estimation. So far, they'd hiked to a beautiful waterfall, eaten at a gourmet restaurant in Little Bavaria, and visited an old German bakery, where they'd feasted on flaky almond croissants and iced bear claws.

"I'd call Owen right now and thank him again if we had cell phone reception," said Alice with a chuckle.

"We'll have to walk over to the rise and call him tomorrow," said Luke. "But meanwhile, it's awfully nice that our phones can't ring."

"Agreed," said Alice.

When they'd wanted to call Alice's parents to let them know they'd arrived safely in Little Bavaria— and found they had no reception—the staff had directed them to take a stroll into the vineyard, where there was a small rise between fields that was pretty much the only place on the grounds from which to make calls. Alice had already noticed the occasional Emmerson staff member hurrying out to that very rise on their break time, and now it all made sense.

"Night's falling fast," said Luke, picking up their honeymoon information packet and checking the schedule. "Time for our romantic walk under the stars."

Alice smiled and took her husband's hand. "Duty calls," she said. "Don't want to keep the photographer waiting."

CHAPTER 2

"Hurry, we're going to be late," said Alice the next day, as she and Luke followed a stone path that led from the inn to the huge barn that had been converted into an event venue.

"Nope," said Luke, taking Alice's hand and pulling her into his arms. "There's no hurrying allowed on this honeymoon."

The previous night's walk under the stars had been amazing. The Emmerson Estate was far enough outside of town that there was little to no light pollution, and the canopy of sky overhead seemed to have layers and layers of stars—millions of them. Even after the photographer had gotten his shots and left,

Alice and Luke had walked on for at least another hour, talking and laughing and making plans.

They'd slept late and enjoyed a leisurely breakfast at the small dining room downstairs, then taken another walk, followed by an indulgent nap before lunchtime. Now, they were about five minutes late for the first official event of the day, a mini wine festival hosted by the Emmersons. The fest was to include the three principle vineyards in the area: the Emmerson Estate Farm and Vineyard, Clear Creek Cellars, and the Waxing Moon Winery.

"I feel kind of bad that I know nothing about wine," Alice said in a low voice as they walked along toward the barn.

"Me, too," said Luke, chuckling. "I know *less* than nothing."

"We can't let anyone know," said Alice. "We have to act sophisticated and knowledgeable. We have to learn the lingo."

When Luke laughed at this, Alice stopped walking. "Seriously! Okay, listen. I learned a new word," she said. "*Oaky*. We're supposed to say wine is oaky if it tastes like an old barrel. Something like that."

"Oaky," Luke repeated.

"Good," said Alice, and they walked on. "Oh—and when they hand us a glass of wine, we're supposed to look straight down into it first, then hold it up to the light, then tilt the glass around a little, then smell it."

"Got it," said Luke. "Thank goodness I married a woman of wisdom."

"Well, in this case, a woman *pretending* to be wise," said Alice with a snicker. "Ooh—hold up." Alice grabbed Luke by the arm and pulled him behind a large flowering bush.

"What—why? Alice, if you want some time alone with me, let's go back to our room."

"Shh! Look over there," said Alice, peeking out from behind the bush to a spot at the side of the barn, where two men stood conversing.

"Okay . . ." said Luke. "What am I looking at?"

"Those two men. Over there. Having a secretive discussion!"

"Alice, you've solved one too many mysteries," said Luke.

It was probably true. Alice, along with Owen and Franny, had helped the police get to the bottom of more than one mystery. Luke and Ben, admittedly, had appreciated their help, but were forever worried about the three amateur sleuths' safety.

"I know body language," said Alice. "And I sense that this is a clandestine meeting. Those two don't want to be disturbed."

"Then let's disturb them and see what happens," said Luke, pulling Alice out of the bush and walking on toward the barn.

By the time they got there, the two men—who didn't look surprised or run off in different directions— simply nodded and kept right on talking as Alice and Luke walked by.

"See?" said Luke. "Nothing secretive about that. Sounded like they were talking about—wait for it —*wine*. Shocking!"

"Okay, okay," said Alice, rolling her eyes. "Let's go inside. We need to pose for a few pictures looking like we love wine."

Maybe Luke was right. Maybe Alice *was* starting to

see mysteries where there were none. Maybe it was time to tone down her constant state of skeptical suspicion. And finally, maybe bad guys weren't actually hiding around every corner, waiting to jump out.

"Alice! Luke! Over here!" Suzie Young called from where she stood next to a long table that had a large banner bearing the Emmerson family crest and distinctive purple lettering.

Alice and Luke had met Suzie and Sam Young on their first day at the inn. The Youngs, also newlyweds, were honeymooning right alongside Alice and Luke, but since they'd bought rather than won their honeymoon package, they weren't required to go to every single fun activity and have their photo taken . . . having fun.

"Hi, Suzie. Sam." Alice nodded at the couple. "Did we miss anything? We're running a little late." She waved at the photographer who smiled and waved back.

"No, they're just getting started. This is going to be so much fun. I can't wait to start tasting the wines."

"Do you know much about wine?" Alice asked casually, hoping Suzie would say yes. Alice figured if

Suzie knew about wine, it would be easy to follow along and do whatever Suzie did.

"As a matter of fact, I do," said Suzie. "We both do." She tilted her head toward her husband.

"You could say wine is our thing," agreed Sam. "We're here to learn everything we can about winemaking."

"Because we're starting our own vineyard!" said Suzie, bursting with excitement. "We already bought some land about an hour from here."

"We gambled everything we have on it. Invested our life savings," added Sam.

"Wow," said Alice. "A true leap of faith, then."

"We want to collect every scrap of information we can find. That's why we chose Emmerson for our honeymoon. They're the best."

"Oh, yes, they are wonderful," said Alice. "We tried their, um, I believe it was their Riesling, last night."

"The Emmerson Riesling is lovely," said Suzie. "Just sweet enough without being too sweet. You know?"

"Very blowsy," agreed Sam.

"Yes," said Luke nodding, a twinkle in his eye as he looked at Alice. "That's just what we were saying. Very blowsy."

"So, what all is happening here at the wine fest today?" asked Alice, changing the subject to keep herself from laughing.

"Start with these," said Suzie, handing Alice and Luke each a very small wine glass engraved with the Emmerson crest. "Now, this table features the Emmerson Estate wines. You can go down the row, read the descriptions, and ask for a taste of any you choose. Then you move on to the next table, which is Clear Creek Cellars, and then finally, to the next one, which is the Waxing Moon Winery."

"You have to pace yourself, I guess," said Luke, raising his eyebrows as he looked down the row of shining bottles.

"Most definitely," said Suzie. "And here." She handed Luke and Alice each a small bottle of water. "Between tastings, sip a little water and eat a cracker, to cleanse you palate." She laughed. "But I'm sure you already know all that."

"Well, we don't get to *that* many wine tastings," said Alice.

"Just be sure to save room for the gourmet lunch they're serving. Oh—and the grand finale, of course."

"What's the grand finale?" asked Alice, hoping it involved chocolate.

"Well, the essencia, of course," said Suzie.

"Oh, good! The *essencia*. That's amazing," said Alice, getting the sense that she should really know what an essencia was.

"At eight hundred dollars a half-bottle, it should be," said Suzie under her breath.

Alice took a sip of water and sputtered a little. "Eight hundred—I mean, yes, but I bet it's going to be a once-in-a-lifetime experience to taste it."

"Once in *our* lifetime for sure," whispered Luke.

"Look!" said Suzie, nodding toward the Clear Creek Cellars table. "There's Forrest Sloan!"

"Oh," said Alice, recognizing the man as one of the two she'd seen talking outside. "I take it he's in the wine business?"

"Are you serious? He's practically a celebrity," said Suzie. "Just as gorgeous in person as he is in the magazines," she whispered, nudging Alice. "He is the grandson of Clear Creek's founder, Elizabeth Emmerson-Sloan."

"Emmerson? As in, these Emmersons here?" asked Alice, pointing at the Emmerson table.

"The very same family," said Suzie, nodding and holding her glass out for a taste of the Emmerson Estate Merlot.

Alice did the same. "So they're all related?" she asked as the attendant poured a sip-sized portion of the deep burgundy liquid into her glass.

Suzie lowered her voice as she swirled her merlot around. "The Emmerson Estate vineyard was founded by a brother and sister. Elizabeth was the sister. I'm not exactly clear about why she split off on her own, but she started Clear Creek just a few miles from here. We'll be over there on Sunday evening, for their annual family festival. It's on your itinerary. "

"And so the Emmersons at this table are related to the Sloans over there?"

"That's right," said Suzie. "But while these two vineyards may *act* like they get along just fine, they're actually arch rivals in the business world."

"What about Waxing Moon over there?" asked Alice, holding her merlot up to the light and peering at it.

"Waxing Moon has a lot of really good offerings," said Suzie. "But they're a distant third. They'd need to come up with something stellar to pull ahead."

"Which is what we're planning to do at our vineyard," said Sam, taking a sip from his glass.

"That's right," said Suzie, giving him a quick peck on the cheek. "We're going to make only a few wines, but make them the best in the industry. We'll be like a boutique vineyard."

Alice took a sip of her wine and coughed a little. "Ah!" she said, recovering quickly. "Very woodsy."

"It *is* woodsy," Sam agreed.

Alice grinned at Luke, who gave her a wink. "Suzie, what is that beautiful jewel I keep seeing on people's lapels?" she asked, nodding toward a young woman at the Emmersons' table, who was chatting with a guest.

"That's the Emmerson crest pendant," said Suzie. "Isn't it glorious? Diamonds and rubies, mostly. Only the family members and a few of the high-up staff get them."

"Gorgeous," said Alice. "So that woman is an Emmerson?"

"Yep. That's Helena. And the man just down from her is her older brother Maximillian. Can you imagine growing up here—being raised in a vineyard? They must know everything there is to know about wine-making. Their grandfather, Walton Emmerson, was the founding brother of this whole estate."

Alice thought about this for a moment. "So they're cousins with the Clear Creek guy? Forrest?"

"Huh. Yes, I suppose they are," said Suzie, holding out her glass to request a taste of the chardonnay.

The tasting went on for the next hour or so, and then everyone was seated at a long, rustic wooden table for a chef-prepared lunch featuring fresh produce from the garden. There were pan-seared scallops with spring onions, baby artichokes, and mushrooms, alongside salads dressed in wine-laced vinaigrette and sprinkled with toasted nuts and goat cheese, and for dessert, crisp pavlova smothered in cream and berries.

Alice was seated next to Luke on one side, and Phillipa Rossi, who happened to be the brand manager at the Waxing Moon Winery, on the other. Phillipa was a kindred spirit—a book lover—and was very excited to find out that Alice owned a bookshop. The two talked about their favorite reads, and about everything from wine and honeymoons.

"Waxing Moon is a great place to work," said Phillipa. "I really believe in our brand. We're not as large as these other vineyards here today, but we have a nice list and some really special bottles." She sighed. "What we need to develop is something akin to Emmerson's essencia. Something spectacular."

"So, tell me about that wine," said Alice. "I hear it's very valuable."

"Oh, yes," said Phillipa, nodding. "It's incredibly rare. And the idea that one could be produced in the Smoky Mountains—well, that's a true miracle. The original essencia comes from one particular region in Hungary. Conditions have to be just right to produce the noble rot."

"*Noble rot?*" Alice made a face.

"Yes, you heard right," said Phillipa, laughing. "It's a particular type of fungus that grows on grapes in moist conditions. Like the mists you see across this vineyard in the mornings."

"Okay," said Alice slowly. "So you need moisture for noble rot to grow."

"Right. But if the moisture goes on too long, the crop is ruined. If it dries up at just the right time, that's when the magic happens. The grapes raisin in the sun with the fungus on them. They have to be hand-picked at exactly the right moment, one at a time."

"So you can't just pick a whole bunch that's got the rot on it?"

"Nope. You have to pick each raisin at exactly the right phase to make an essencia. And then those raisins are put into barrels and are pressed naturally, by their own weight, for oh, about eight years."

"Eight years!" said Alice.

"But what you are left with is pure magic," said Phillipa.

Alice watched as the servers moved down the table, taking away dessert plates and replacing them with a single crystal spoon at each place. Alice looked at her spoon—which was also engraved with the Emmerson crest. "What's this for?" she asked.

"Essencia is not taken in a glass," said Phillipa. "We'll each get one heavenly spoonful only."

"Seriously?"

"Just wait," said Phillipa with a grin.

As they waited for the essencia to be poured into the crystal spoons, Alice noticed the man she'd seen talking to Forrest Sloan outside earlier. Now that he was closer at hand, Alice could see that along with his very dashing suit, he wore a small silver cup on a chain around his neck.

"Phillipa, why is that man wearing that strange necklace?" Alice asked.

Phillipa looked in the direction Alice was looking and giggled. "That's Rupert Billings. He's our lead sommelier at Waxing Moon—an award-winning sommelier, actually. The necklace is called a tastevin. Sommeliers use them to sample wines as they walk through the barrel rooms. Really, these days the tastevin is more of a symbol, but all Waxing Moon sommeliers wear them."

"And a sommelier is . . ."

"A wine steward. They create wine lists at restaurants, suggest wine pairings . . . they are experts in the field, and a great one on the scale of Rupert Billings is a rare find. We're lucky to have him."

Alice watched as Rupert leaned closer to Helena Emmerson, who he was seated next to, to say something quietly—then noticed that Helena blushed, a small smile touching her lips.

Alice turned to Luke. "Just to show you how good I am at reading body language, how much do you want to bet those two are in love?" she whispered.

"Those two?" Luke whispered back, looking at Rupert and Helena. He chuckled. "How can you possibly tell? I think the romance of this place has gotten to you, my love."

"No, I can always tell when love is in the air," said Alice sighing. "You'll see."

"It's the big moment," Phillipa whispered from Alice's other side. "Time to taste the essencia!"

After a few words from Maximillian Emmerson, everyone raised their crystal spoons and drank the wine. Alice was astonished as her tongue was coated in sweetness. The magical substance had the consistency of honey, and flavor unlike anything Alice had ever experienced—and yet it was familiar.

"Figs? Plums?" Alice wondered.

"I was thinking something like sweet orange," said Luke. "But whatever it is, this stuff is amazing."

Suzie, who was seated across the table with Sam, caught Alice's attention. "What did I tell you?" she said giddily, still savoring the flavor of her spoonful. "To die for!"

CHAPTER 3

Friday was to be rounded out by a sunset hot air balloon ride, which took off from the vineyard, circled out over the woods and the village of Little Bavaria, then returned to the vineyard. Alice, having never been in a hot air balloon before, was a little nervous at the prospect. The *Fabulous Bride Magazine* photographer was also, apparently, hesitant to launch himself thousands of feet in the air, so he snapped his photos of Alice and Luke waving from the edge of the basket as they lifted off. Thankfully, as it turned out, Alice loved the sensation of floating silently above the trees, drifting along on the breeze.

The balloon operator, George, turned out to be a big part of what made the experience so enjoyable.

Between presenting Alice and Luke with a basket of fine chocolates, cheeses, and grapes, pouring glasses of sweet red port, and telling stories about the things they were seeing on the ground, George managed to relate a lot of the history of the area vineyards.

"I can't believe we get our own private balloon tour," said Luke. "This is amazing."

"Actually," said George, "there was supposed to be another honeymoon couple here with us. The Youngs?"

"Suzie and Sam!" said Alice. "We've met them."

"They cancelled last minute," said George. "So you have the sky all to yourselves. Feel free to ask me anything about what you're seeing on the ground."

"What can you tell us about the two Emmerson siblings who founded the vineyard?" asked Alice, remembering her conversation with Suzie.

"Ah! That would be Elizabeth and Walton." George turned on one of the burners and the balloon rose a little higher in the air.

"What were they like?" asked Luke.

"Like-minded in almost every way. They both had the gift for winemaking. It was as though they were born to it. They bought the original land together, and slowly added on and developed their wines over the next few decades."

"So, why did Elizabeth leave?"

"She married Oliver Sloan. He and Walton didn't get along. Elizabeth and Oliver decided to branch out, so they sold Elizabeth's interest in the Emmerson Estate and bought a nearby vineyard that was struggling from a lack of capital. They transformed it, and called it Clear Creek Cellars."

"Does Clear Creek make an essencia wine like Emmerson?" asked Alice.

"There's the rub!" said George, chuckling. "No— Clear Creek has never mastered a viable formula. But you see, the two vineyards didn't start out as rivals. Sure, Elizabeth and her husband decided to create their own brand. But there were no hard feelings, really, between the Emmerson siblings. Then, just before the split took place, Elizabeth had come up with the idea of creating an essencia based on the original, which was created in Hungary. Walton agreed to the idea, because the conditions at the Emmerson estate are unique, even to this region—and conducive to the mysterious and elusive noble rot. After Elizabeth went her own way, Walton assembled a team at his vineyard who landed on a winning formula—and that formula is guarded under lock and key."

"So, the rivalry between the vineyards arose because the essencia was Elizabeth's idea, but Walton's formula," said Luke. "And Walton had not desired to share his secret."

"Exactly," said George. "Now, Emmerson is famous for that wine, and it's set them a bit ahead in the game —that and the fact that the Emmerson vineyard was already established before Elizabeth and Oliver Sloan really managed to get Clear Creek off the ground. There's definitely some lingering resentment in the air between the two."

"We tried the essencia last night," said Alice. "We've never experienced anything like it."

"It's quite unique," said George, nodding. He turned off both of the burners and the balloon began to sink slowly as they came to the edge of the Emmerson estate, nearing their journey's end. "It's actually made from a combination of three sweet grapes. Of course, I don't know the ratios or the formula, but I can tell you that those grapes right down there—the yellow Muscat—are one of the three varieties the Emmersons use to make their essencia."

A sudden gust of wind swept in, carrying the balloon a bit higher.

"What was that?" asked Alice, gripping the sides of the basket.

"Just a bit of a breeze," said George as he took hold of one of the ropes that seemed to steer the balloon. "Bad timing. I was just lining up for our landing field." He turned various levers on and off. "Luke, can you pull on this chord while I let a little bit of air out?"

"Sure," said Luke, moving to George's side of the balloon basket.

"Don't worry, we'll get down safely," said George, giving Alice a comforting smile.

Alice nodded and focused on the ground beneath them. She watched as row after row of Emmerson grapes passed by under them in the dusky evening light, trying not to imagine the balloon being swept suddenly up into the stratosphere, never to return to *terra firma.*

A sudden movement and a swatch of dark color caught Alice's eye. Down there, between the two rows of grapevines which were now directly beneath the balloon, she saw it: two people fighting—a man with dark hair wearing the Emmerson colors of deep purple and golden brown and another man in what looked like a black sweat suit with a hood.

"Oh, my gosh!" Alice glanced for a split second at Luke, then looked down again, just in time to see the two men fall onto the ground, fists flying. Alice thought she heard the faint sound of a shot being fired, and the two grew still. Then the hooded figure slowly rose, while the other man lay motionless as the balloon passed over high above. "Luke! Hurry!"

"Alice. What is it?" Luke crossed back over to Alice's side, jiggling the basket.

"Down there. Can you see the person—I mean . . . Where are they now?"

"Where are who?" asked Luke, frowning down at the

ground.

"There was a man—he was shot! Oh my gosh! We have to get down there!"

"Shot? Alice, are you sure?"

"Yes! Between the rows, over that way." Alice quickly tried to memorize the topography, although they were well past being able to see between the two particular rows where the shooting had happened. She saw a large rock at the end of the rows nearby. "George, how fast can you get us down?"

"I'm on it," said George, reaching up and pulling on a chord that caused air to leave the balloon.

They sank slowly as they moved along the ground, aiming for the same open field they'd launched from. As soon as they landed, George hopped out of the balloon and hooked a small stepladder onto the outside of the basket. Alice and Luke scurried up the small steps inside the basket and then down the ladder outside.

"We have to hurry!" said Alice, feeling her heart pounding out of her chest. "The person in black will get away!"

Luke and George ran along with Alice until she stopped and looked around, disoriented. "Where is that big stone?" she mumbled.

"We came across the vines from that direction," said George.

They all ran where George was pointing, and jogged down row after row, looking down each of them while also searching for the large stone Alice had seen.

"Alice, it's getting dark," said Luke. "Are you sure it's this way?"

Alice squinted up ahead and spotted a large stone. "This way!" she said. "I saw that stone from the balloon."

When they arrived at the stone, they turned and ran down the row of vines. Alice stopped and looked around. Luke and George stopped, too. There was no sound, save the chirping of crickets, tuning up for their evening concert. There was no sign of another person—no sign that anyone had passed this way recently. Alice squinted at the ground, looking for blood or footprints or anything at all . . .

"Luke, I know what I saw," she said, still catching her breath.

"And what, exactly, was that?" asked Luke.

"There was a person dressed in black. They had a hood on, so I couldn't tell what they looked like or even for sure whether they were male or female. That person was fighting with a man with dark hair, dressed in an Emmerson uniform. They were sort of rolling around on the ground, and then I think I heard a shot fired. Then the person in black stood up, holding a gun, and the man in the Emmerson uniform stayed on the ground. Luke, he was so still. I think he was dead." She looked at her husband. "I swear, I saw it, Luke." She scanned the ground. "Look, the grass is matted down over there. Maybe that's where it happened."

"I'm calling the police," said George. "But I'll have to go over to the rise to get any reception at all. You stay here so we don't lose our place."

After George had run off, Alice turned to Luke, shaking her head, and beginning to feel her whole body tremble. "I know what I saw. Someone died here tonight."

CHAPTER 4

Since the Emmerson estate was a bit of a drive from town, it took the police a while to arrive. By the time the cruiser, which had turned off its siren upon entering the estate, pulled up, a small crowd had gathered in the vineyard. The group was comprised of George, Alice, and Luke, along with several Emmerson staff members and Maximillian Emmerson himself. Alice had caught sight of Suzie and Sam standing and watching curiously from a distance, but a moment later, she looked back and they were gone.

The uniformed officer quickly hopped out of the cruiser and set up a bright light in the area where Alice had seen the shooting take place. A second officer walked up and down the rows of vines with a flashlight and a German shepherd. A man wearing khakis and a button-down introduced himself as Detective Mullins and interviewed Alice, Luke, and George, taking notes and looking more and more skeptical as time went on.

"Mrs. Evans, the balloon was pretty high when you say you saw the hooded person shoot the person in the Emmerson uniform. Are you absolutely certain you saw what you think you saw? Could it have been a trick of the light?"

"No, that's not possible," said Alice, confused by the question. "I can't imagine that the light would have any effect on what I saw."

"And you say you saw a confrontation taking place, but you heard nothing? No yelling? No screaming?"

"I might've heard the gunshot," said Alice.

"Might have?"

"It was faint. We were up pretty high and the balloon was making a lot of noise at the moment, plus there was wind."

"And neither of you saw this shooting take place or heard anything?" the detective asked, turning to Luke and George, who both shook their heads with apologetic glances toward Alice.

"We were on the other side of the balloon basket, sir," said Luke.

"There had been a sudden gust, and Mr. Evans was helping me keep the balloon on course," added George.

"When Alice saw the shooting take place—and I assure you, Detective Mullins, my wife knows what she saw—we hurried over but it was too late. We'd already drifted past the vantage point."

Helena Emmerson, who had been present earlier, but had left after conferring quietly with the detective and Maximillian, returned just then. "We checked in with every member of the staff. They're all accounted for," she said.

"Boys, pack it up," Detective Mullins said to the two uniformed officers.

"What? Now?" Alice blurted out, surprised. "But you haven't found any clues yet. Are you coming back in the morning?"

Detective Mullins stepped closer to Alice. "Mrs.

Evans, had you been drinking before seeing what you claim to have seen?"

Alice hesitated. "We'd had a small glass of wine with our cheese and chocolate," she said. "Detective, I don't know what you're implying, but—"

"I'm not implying anything, Mrs. Evans. You say you saw a shooting from a hot air balloon, but you aren't even sure you heard a shot being fired, and no one else saw anything. You say the victim was wearing the very distinctive Emmerson vineyard uniform, but no staff member is missing. You say this shooting took place here, among these vines . . . " He pointed to the rows of vines near the large stone. "But there is no blood and—oh yeah—no *body*!"

"What about that area over there, where the grass is all pressed down?" asked Alice.

"This area right here?" Detective Mullins walked briskly to where Alice was pointing. "This grass?"

Alice nodded.

"Come closer, Mrs. Evans," said Mullins.

When Alice walked to where he was standing, he squatted near the tamped-down grass. "See this here

—this fuzzy stuff caught in this grapevine? That's the hair of a white-tailed deer. See those droppings over there? Same. If someone had been shot here, there would be blood. The dog would smell it. Now. Rest assured, Mrs. Evans, that if we collect any viable evidence, we will thoroughly investigate this matter. Meanwhile, you should concentrate on enjoying your vacation." He gave her a curt nod and walked off.

Alice could feel her cheeks burning and was glad it was too dark for anyone else to notice her face turning red. Then she got mad at herself for feeling embarrassed. She'd done nothing wrong, after all, and what kind of person would she be had she not reported what she saw? If someone had actually been shot, they'd be missed eventually, and the burden of responsibility to find the killer would rest on the shoulders of Detective Mullins and his crew. Alice was on her honeymoon. Her only responsibility was to enjoy herself.

Luke took her hand. "Don't worry, my love," he whispered. "The police will investigate more when something turns up."

They started walking back toward the inn.

"But what if nothing turns up?" asked Alice.

"If someone was shot, something will turn up," Luke assured her. "Hey—it couldn't have been that you saw some kids playing cops and robbers, could it?"

Alice stopped walking. "I hadn't thought of that. Maybe. No. I don't think so. But maybe."

"Well I'm glad you're so sure of that," Luke said with a chuckle.

Alice sighed and looked up at the starry sky. "Let's just get back to the honeymooning business, okay?"

Luke leaned in to kiss her, but her cell phone rang. "Oh. Ha! Look at that! We're standing on the rise," said Alice, taking the phone out of her bag. "It's Owen!"

Actually, it turned out to be both Owen and Franny, who were calling Alice on speakerphone. Alice switched her phone speaker on as well, so that Luke could join the conversation.

"So, how's life in paradise?" asked Owen.

"It's amazing—or, it was amazing. There was a little glitch, but now it's amazing again," said Alice, laughing at herself. "I thought I saw a murder happen while we were on our sunset hot air balloon ride."

"You *what*?" said Owen. There was a scuffling sound. "Sorry, Alice. I dropped the phone. I thought you said—"

"That *is* what I said. I thought I saw someone get shot in the vineyard . . . from about a thousand feet overhead. But the police don't believe me, and Luke didn't see it happen, and I really just wish you guys were here."

"Well, we *are* a crime-solving machine when we're together," said Owen.

"Alice, we believe you!" Franny called, and baby Theo gurgled in the background.

"Is that my favorite nephew I hear?" asked Alice. "Hi Theo! Aunt Alice and Uncle Luke miss you!" And it was true. Alice loved this haven she and Luke had found, but standing on the rise, hearing the voices of her friends, her family, she felt a pang of homesickness that surprised her. She suddenly longed to be sitting in their rooftop garden, drinking a glass of wine, and talking about her day at the bookshop with Owen and Franny.

After they hung up, she took Luke's arm and they walked on toward the inn. As they came to the last rows of grapevines before the land gave way to the gardens and the yard, Alice saw something move in her peripheral vision. She stopped and turned to see Helena Emmerson, standing off to the side in the shadows, crying quietly.

She leaned close to Luke. "If nothing is wrong, then why is Helena crying?"

CHAPTER 5

Alice and Luke had fallen into bed the night before, exhausted. When the golden sunlight filtered through the sheer curtains the next morning, Alice found that she felt better. Refreshed. Relieved that all she had to do that day was spend time with the man she loved in this beautiful place. She smelled something wonderful coming from the dining room downstairs and smiled.

"Smells like fresh bread," she said to Luke as he sleepily sat up in bed.

"Makes me wish Owen was here," said Luke. "As amazing as the food is, he could still show the chef a thing or two down in the kitchen. Nobody's better at bread than Owen."

"He can probably sense you just said that all the way from Blue Valley," said Alice. "I can almost imagine him gloating, even from here."

They stretched and yawned and dressed, and then headed downstairs, following the wonderful smells of breakfast. They could hear voices and the soft clinks of glasses and silverware.

"Anyway," Alice heard one diner saying, "that's how you get an airier texture in your bread. It's foolproof and it works, no matter the weather."

"Wait. That sounded like—" Alice stopped walking and looked at Luke, who looked right back at her.

"Now, if you want to talk *cakes*, I have a million—"

"Owen!" Alice had spotted him by this time. He was sitting in the dining room, the head chef seated next to him taking notes. At Owen's other elbow was Franny. "Franny!"

Alice ran to the table just as her brother, Ben, returned from the lavish buffet with a plate full of food.

"Ben! You're all here!"

Owen and Franny jumped up and surrounded Alice in a hug.

"We couldn't stay away," said Owen. "We could tell on the phone last night that you needed us."

"Hope this isn't too weird," said Ben, shaking hands with Luke. "I have the next few days off and couldn't resist a little getaway with Franny. We haven't had that since Theo was born." He chuckled and looked at Alice. "Between Mom and Dad and Franny's parents, Theo is going to have the time of his life while we're away."

"Weird?" said Luke with a laugh. "This is the opposite of weird. For us, *this* is normal."

"He makes a good point," said Owen. "And don't worry—we won't interfere in your honeymoon romance one bit. We're just here to have a relaxing weekend, and if we solve the thing about Alice seeing the guy get shot in the vineyard, well, that's just icing on the cake. Oh!" Owen looked back at the chef, who was standing next to the table. "Chef Bruno, let's get together in the kitchen later, when we can exchange ideas and recipes."

Chef Bruno gladly agreed and hurried off to the kitchen.

"I'm starved," said Alice, eyeing the buffet. "Let's eat breakfast and then take a walk. I'll tell you the whole story. Oh—and our fun activity per *Fabulous Bride Magazine* this morning is miniature golf in Little Bavaria. You're all coming."

After a decadent breakfast of strawberry-laden French toast drizzled in warm maple syrup and melted butter, along with a cup of hot coffee, Alice felt very ready for a nice, long walk around the estate. She and Luke showed the others around—where the apple blossoms were prettiest, where the trail veered off to the lake, where the fresh produce in the kitchen came from, and where the cell phone-reception rise lay.

"So, you were on your hot air balloon ride . . ." Ben said when there was a pause in the conversation.

Alice nodded. "At dusk. Last night. We were drifting back toward the vineyard on the return trip. We were still up pretty high—but not that high, because we were going to be landing soon."

"There was a little gust of wind," said Luke. "And George, our pilot, asked me to help him. So he and I were distracted with that while Alice was looking down at the ground on the other side of the basket."

"And what, exactly, did you see?" asked Ben. Alice half expected him to take out the little notebook and pen he always carried when investigating at work.

"A person in a dark-colored hoodie . . . either black or midnight blue . . . and a person wearing an Emmerson Estate uniform—you saw them at the inn, with the deep purple vest and the golden brown tie."

When everyone nodded, Alice continued. "They were standing in one of these rows of vines." She swept an arm out over the vineyard that lay before them. "They got into a fight and at some point, the person in the hood shot the Emmerson person. I just saw the gun in the hooded person's hand, and I saw the Emmerson person lying on the ground motionless. Then the balloon drifted past, and I couldn't see them anymore. It all happened so fast. The light wasn't good. I couldn't hear anything, because we were still too high up and George was using the balloon equipment, which can be noisy at times."

"So, you landed, and then what?" asked Owen.

"I had remembered there was a large stone near the area where the shooting took place. So we ran out into the vines and found the stone and then looked all around that area. Nothing but deer poop."

"Deer poop?" asked Franny.

"White-tailed deer poop," said Alice, nodding sadly. "The police came, and there was no body, no blood, no evidence, and no one missing from the Emmerson staff. So basically they thought I was crazy."

"Are you sure you were looking in the right place?" asked Owen. "Things look different from above."

"We'll have to figure that out later," said Luke, looking at his watch. "We're expected at the miniature golf course in Little Bavaria in half an hour."

"Oh, um, well, you two have a great time," said Owen.

"Oh, no you don't," said Alice. "You won this honeymoon for us, Owen. You should all come, too."

"Yeah, we wouldn't want you to miss out on any of the fun," said Luke, chuckling. "Let's all go."

"I'm up for it if we can make it a tournament," said Franny. "I like to win."

"This woman has a competitive streak like no one else," said Ben, slinging an arm around Franny.

"Are you kidding? I've seen her in the Blue Lake Fourth of July Paddleboat Regatta!" said Alice. "And Owen was her cohort."

"They did beat you two," said Luke.

"That was two summers ago!" said Alice. "Ben and I beat them last year."

"And we'll prevail again this year," said Ben.

"Bring it on, Maguire!" said Owen.

"Let's hit the golf course," said Franny. "A little friendly competition never hurt anyone."

CHAPTER 6

The Little Bavaria Putt Haus Mini-Golf Fun Zone turned out to be quite an adventure. The most challenging hole was a toss-up between the Giant Pretzel and the unique Wurst Windmill . . . not to be outdone by the formidable Zugspitze Challenge, which involved getting your ball to go up the side of the snow-capped mountain, where it landed in a tiny roller coaster that then carried it down the other side and popped it into the hole.

"Yes! I am the champion!" said Franny as the last ball in the group fell short of her extraordinary hole in one. Franny was awarded a small trophy which was topped with a gleaming golden sausage link, the emblem of the Putt Haus.

The whole group headed back to the vineyard for lunch, which was being served in the barn that day. Everyone went to their rooms to freshen up, and then met out in the yard, where they walked along the stone path, following the delicious aroma of food.

As they neared the barn, still chatting about everything from golf to gourmet cooking, Alice heard the distinct sound of an anguished sob. She looked up and saw Helena, standing off to the side of the barn. When Helena saw them, she motioned for them to come over to where she was.

"I've been waiting for you," she said, wiping her eyes with a tissue.

Alice introduced Helena to Owen, Franny, and Ben. "What's wrong, Helena?"

"I need to know—I mean, can you please tell me about the person you saw in the vineyard yesterday? The person you saw get shot?" Her voice cracked on this last sentence and tears overflowed from her eyes again.

"Well," said Alice, "the person was a man. Wearing a uniform like the other Emmerson staff members. He had dark hair. Fairly tall. It was hard to tell from above. I couldn't see any details at all."

"I, um, have a friend I'm concerned about . . . I haven't heard from him since yesterday, and I'm worried. You've seen him before. He was at the wine tasting. He's the sommelier, from Waxing Moon? Rupert Billings? I—" A small sob escaped her. "I'm afraid it was him you saw."

"But Helena, the person I saw was clearly wearing an Emmerson uniform." Alice thought for a moment. "I supposed if it weren't for that, though, it could have been Rupert."

Helena blew her nose. "I know it was him! I just know it!"

"You poor girl," Owen said, patting Helena on the shoulder. "It's going to be okay. Is there someone we can call?" He glanced at Alice, his eyes hopeful that she could think of some way to help.

"I know! I'll call Phillipa Rossi," said Alice. "We bonded over books at the wine tasting. She's the brand manager at Waxing Moon. We exchanged contact information."

Alice took out her phone and called Phillipa, and asked her about whether the sommelier had been to work lately.

"Funny you should ask that," said Phillipa. "We're worried sick. He didn't come in last night or this morning. Weekends are our busiest time. Rupert would never miss a Saturday at work without calling in."

When Alice hung up with Phillipa, she turned somber eyes to Helena. "He hasn't been in—not last night, and not this morning. And he hasn't called."

"No!" cried Helena. She looked at Alice. "Tell me again where and when you saw the shooting."

Alice described where she thought it had happened, and when was easy, because George had known exactly what time it was when they'd started their descent in the balloon. He'd said sunset was at precisely 8:07 that day, and Alice had reported seeing the shooting about ten minutes later.

Helena nodded sadly, thanked Alice, and hurried away.

"So sad," said Franny.

"But it looks like you really saw something happen out in the vineyard after all," said Ben.

"And it also shows that I was right about Helena and Rupert being involved," said Alice, raising a brow at Luke.

"Okay, I admit it," he said. "You do know body language."

They headed into the barn, where tables were scattered about with jars of wildflowers in their centers. They were seated and served thick sandwiches on homemade bread, crispy seasoned house potato chips, fresh fruit, iced minted tea, and sparkling wine. Dessert was a giant, gooey chocolate chip cookie for each person.

"We're going to have to walk a few extra miles when we get home," said Owen, patting his stomach as they left the barn.

"No kidding," said Alice, wishing her pants had an elastic waistband.

"Hey—looks like the police are back," said Luke. "Let's go see what they're up to."

Sure enough, a couple of police cruisers were parked

in the lot along with an ambulance. Detective Mullens was standing in the parking lot, holding his cell phone up in the air and looking frustrated.

"Oh, Detective Mullens, there's no reception here," said Alice, hurrying over to him. "You have to go to that little rise in the land over there. I can show you."

"You," said Mullens. "Mrs. Evans, correct?"

Alice nodded.

"Was it you who called us?" he asked.

"What? Today, you mean? No."

Luke joined them, along with the others. "Afternoon, Detective Mullens."

"Detective Evans," said Mullens, nodding.

"I'd like you to meet my brother-in-law, Ben Maguire. He's the police captain in Blue Valley. This is his wife Franny and our friend Owen James."

Mullens nodded at each of them and they all walked toward the rise.

"So what brings you back to the vineyard?" asked Luke.

"We got an anonymous call," said Mullens. "A woman's voice, calling from here." He eyed Alice.

"I assure you, Detective, I didn't make that call," said Alice.

When his eyes shifted to Franny, she looked surprised. "Neither did I," she said, holding up her hands. "We've all been together at lunch."

"Any new information about the shooting Alice saw?" asked Luke.

"Oh, we found something new, all right," said Mullens, stopping at the rise and trying his phone again. "If you'll excuse me, I have a call to make. You're not leaving town, are you? We may have further questions for you later."

"Nope. We'll be here," said Luke. "If you don't mind my asking, what is the new thing you found?"

Mullens didn't answer this, but looked toward the rows of vines, where the paramedics were emerging with a stretcher . . . and on the stretcher was a covered body.

"The gunshot victim, I presume," said Owen, giving

the detective a look of disdain. "The one Alice saw that no one believed her about."

"Where did you find the victim?" asked Ben.

Begrudgingly, Mullens said, "Back of the vineyard, in the woods. Someone had hurriedly buried him."

"Him?" asked Alice. "What's his name?"

"Don't leave town," Mullens said sternly, and turned away to make his call.

Alice hurried over to the parking lot, where the paramedics were loading the body into the ambulance. "Excuse me, is that Rupert Billings?" she asked.

One of the paramedics stopped and turned to Alice, a look of compassion on his face. "I'm so sorry, ma'am. Did you know him?"

CHAPTER 7

The *Fabulous Bride Magazine* photographer had just finished taking shots of Alice and Luke gazing at one another during their Moonlit Picnic Among the Vines.

"You can come out now," Alice called. There was a pause, and then Owen, Franny, and Ben emerged from behind a clump of bushes.

"We just wanted to see how the photo shoot was going," said Owen, snickering.

"You looked so in love," said Franny with a happy sigh.

"We *are* so in love," said Alice, rolling her eyes.

"Now get over here. They gave us a ridiculous amount of food. You have to eat some."

"That's the thing about the magazine photos," said Luke. "They want to make everything look so lavish that they order way too much food for two people. We've been trying to get the photographer to help us eat it, but he's got all kinds of food allergies, so he's been no help at all."

"Sit," said Alice, scooting closer to Luke to make more room on the picnic blanket.

"This looks amazing," said Ben, helping himself to one of the wrapped roast beef sandwiches from the overflowing picnic basket.

"Try the roasted vegetable and orzo salad," said Alice. "It's amazing."

"Wow, the roast chicken is out of this world," said Franny. "That Chef Bruno knows his stuff!"

"He's definitely got potential in the baking department," Owen agreed, inspecting a mini cherry tart.

Everyone dug in, and Luke poured the champagne. In the quiet of the moment, they heard voices coming from nearby.

"Did you hear that?" whispered Alice.

"Shh!" said Owen. "I think it's that Helena from earlier."

"Well I'm *glad* he's dead," said a male voice, drifting over the vines.

"Max, how can you say that?" asked Helena.

Alice's eyes widened. "It's Maximilian and Helena Emmerson. They're brother and sister," she whispered. "They own this place."

"He was using you, Helena," said Max.

"I know," she admitted in return. "He didn't want me. He wanted that stupid essencia formula. But Max, if the police find out about the fight I had with Rupert just before he died, they'll think I killed him."

"Then they'd better not find out."

"So, Rupert was after the secret to the essencia!" whispered Alice.

"Max, I was right there, over near the woods where he died," Helena went on. "What if they find, like, DNA evidence or something?"

"What were you doing over there anyway?" asked Max, clearly frustrated with his sister.

"That's where we always met. It's . . . private there." She sighed. "By the big stone, near the tree line."

"I *knew* there was a big stone," whispered Alice.

"Shh!" said Owen.

"Well, apparently, Rupert met more people than just you there, Helena. I can't believe you let him use one of our uniforms."

"Sometimes he snuck in to see me in the evenings after work," said Helena. "He didn't want anyone to notice him."

"Everyone is after that formula," said Max. "I knew Clear Creek would kill to get their hands on it. But not Waxing Moon! I thought we were safe around them. And I assume they have the secret now. I mean, the formula wasn't found on Rupert's body. I checked with Detective Mullins. So the killer must've taken it from him. We're not going to be the only essencia game in town anymore."

"No—Rupert would never have written the formula down," said Helena. "The man was a genius with a photographic memory. It's part of why he was so gifted as a sommelier. I promise you, he found the formula and memorized it."

"And how, I wonder, did he find out where we keep the formula?" asked Max, a note of scathing sarcasm in his voice.

"Max, he'd asked me to marry him! I'd said yes! I thought he was going to be joining our family. I—I was so stupid."

There was a pause. "Oh Helena. I'm sorry." Alice guessed Max was hugging his sister now, because her sobs were muffled. "That jerk broke your heart."

The two must've moved back toward the inn, because their voices faded after that. But Alice heard Max mumbling, "Rupert Billings got what was coming to him."

"Well." Owen took a big bite of the cherry tart and wiped his fingers with a napkin. "This place is a regular soap opera. I take that back, it's more like a mini-series. This is prime time stuff. And we have two viable suspects."

"True," said Luke. "Both Helena and Max had motive to kill Rupert. She'd been wronged by him. Betrayed. And Max would've been furious when he found out Rupert had stolen the family secret."

"Plus, he'd be mad Rupert hurt his kid sister," Ben said, elbowing Alice.

"But I'm pretty sure Helena was the one who called the police. If she was the killer, she surely wouldn't have done that," said Alice.

"Unless she was suddenly overwhelmed with guilt for what she'd done," said Franny. "She did, after all, just have a terrible fight with Rupert by her own admission."

"And the fight took place right where the police found the body," added Ben.

"Is there anyone else we can add to the list of suspects?" asked Owen. "Anyone else who'd kill for the secret to that crazy-expensive wine?"

Everyone thought for a moment.

"Oh!" Alice suddenly perked up. "How about someone who is just getting started in the wine-making business and needs a showstopper?"

Luke looked at her. "You mean the Youngs? Suzie and Sam?"

Alice nodded.

"Come to think of it, they do have everything riding on the success of their little vineyard venture."

"And I did see them hanging around when the police were here just after I saw Rupert get shot," said Alice.

They filled Owen, Franny, and Ben in on the Youngs, and all were in agreement that if the Youngs had somehow known what Rupert was up to in stealing the formula for the essencia, one of them might've approached him.

"That could be the real reason they're here," said Owen. "Maybe the honeymoon is just a ruse, and they came to steal that formula. But when the sassy sommelier beat them to it, they went after him instead."

"It's possible," said Luke.

"We can try to find out more in the morning," said Alice, opening the picnic basket and starting to load up the leftovers. "Suzie told me they'd be at our first fun activity of the day." She put air quotes around "fun."

"What's that?" asked Owen.

"Zip lining," said Alice.

"As in, going up high and careening toward the ground at top speed on a thin wire?" asked Owen.

"That's right," said Alice, raising a brow at Owen. "All the fabulous brides are doing it. We need to be there at nine. Be sure to set your alarms."

CHAPTER 8

"For the love of humanity, who is Old Johnny, and why does he hate me?" Owen peered up into the treetops, where helmeted zip liners balanced precariously on wooden platforms while they were snapped into harnesses and then sent whizzing from tree to tree.

But Old Johnny's Adventure Park featured more than just zip lining.

"Look! There's a wobbly suspension bridge!" said Franny, pointing up.

"And a ropes course," said Ben. "That'll be a challenge."

The *Fantastic Bride Magazine* photographer had arrived just after them and stood looking dubiously upward.

"Come on, my groom," said Alice. "We'd better get up there."

Alice, Luke, and company climbed up the ladder to the wooden platform, to a ride Old Johnny had dubbed the "Lily-Liver's Special." Once on the platform, Old Johnny's hillbilly voice could be heard over a hidden speaker saying, "Take this ride just so's you can say you zip lined—you scaredy-cats!" followed by a cackle.

"Are there going to be insulting recordings of Old Johnny on every one of these attractions?" asked Owen, tightening up his helmet.

"Try standing here all day, hearing him say that again and again," said the ride attendant who, according to his name tag, was named Erwin Swanson.

"So, Erwin, has anyone ever—I don't know—*died* on this zip line?" asked Owen.

"Not on the Lily-Liver," said Erwin, shaking his head.

"What are you saying, Erwin?" asked Alice. "That people *have* died on some of these other challenges?"

"Could you two smile? And how about if all your friends laugh as though having the time of their lives?" said the *Fabulous Bride* photographer. "I'm afraid of heights, and I'm most definitely going to barf if I don't get down from here soon."

Alice and Luke quickly looked at each other, smiling as though they couldn't wait to fly through the trees harnessed together like two lovebirds, while Owen, Ben, and Franny tossed back their heads and laughed joyfully. Once the photos were snapped, the photographer made a hasty exit and Owen broke out in a cold sweat.

"Do we have to do this?" he asked.

"Yes, and I'll tell you why," said Alice, nodding across the trees to another platform in the distance. "There are the Youngs up ahead of us. This is the only way to get to them fast, before they move out of our sight and we lose them. Now get that harness on and act casual."

"I don't know how casual I can act while plummeting

to my death, but I'll try," said Owen, taking a deep breath. "Strap me in, Erwin Swanson."

A few seconds later, Alice and Luke were flying through the air. In the course of the short ride, Alice felt laughter bubbling up in her heart, and then saw that Luke was laughing too. It was the most invigorating thing Alice had ever experienced. The attendant at the next landing platform caught them and helped them prepare for the following line. Alice could hear Owen shrieking in the distance behind them, and then Franny's loud *whoop*. But by the time they landed, Alice and Luke were whizzing on down the next line. Finally, they landed at a treetop cabana, where zip liners could stop and enjoy snacks and drinks while taking in the glorious view or watching others sailing along through the branches.

"Pull up a chair and sit yerself down," said another recording of Old Johnny. "Grab one of our famous fried pies or a milkshake!"

"I am *not* eating a fried pie if I have to do any more zip lining today," said Owen, plopping into a chair at one of the empty tables. "Not today, Old Johnny!"

"Don't worry," said Alice, sitting next to Owen. "We'll be using that stairway to get down from here. No more zip lining."

"The Youngs are right over there," said Luke. "Let's wave them over."

A few minutes later, Sam and Suzie had taken seats at the table, and a few minutes after that, sizzling fried pies in little tissue paper-lined baskets were delivered to the table.

"These look delicious," said Suzie, blowing on hers. "And by the way, it's so great that all your friends are here!"

Alice had already introduced Sam and Suzie to Owen, Franny, and Ben.

"We're here on the same honeymoon package as Alice and Luke," Suzie told the group. "But we haven't been doing all the schedule activities. Like this afternoon, we're skipping out and staying around the vineyard to see what else we can learn about winemaking."

"Congratulations on getting married," said Franny.

"Sam and Suzie are going to be starting up their own vineyard," said Alice.

"Wow, that's amazing!" said Owen, acting surprised. "Sounds risky."

"Well, we're risk-takers," said Suzie, eyeing the next zip liners who were just coming in for a landing. "And we're wine lovers, too." She took a big bite of her fried pie and closed her eyes. "Mmm. Peach."

"So, did you hear about the murder at the vineyard?" asked Alice.

"Yes, we did," said Suzie, her face clouding over.

"Terrible," said Franny, shaking her head.

"I heard it was that guy—the sommelier from Waxing Moon Winery—who got shot," said Alice, leaning in closer.

"We did too," said Sam, taking a bite of pie. "So sad."

Suzie popped the last bite of her peach pie into her mouth and wiped her fingers on her napkin. "Well, we'd better be going," she said, standing.

Sam stood too. "We're headed over to the Cattywampus Catastrophe zip line next. It's going to be wild! You in?"

"Oh, I think we'll sit here and eat pie for a while yet," said Alice. "Um, just wondering . . ." Alice fished around in her mind for a way to quickly stop the Youngs from rushing off and get back to the subject of the murder. "Do you two feel perfectly safe? I mean, over at the vineyard? Knowing there's a murderer on the loose?"

Suzie smiled. "Absolutely. I mean, that wasn't just some random killing. Rupert Billings got himself into trouble, and he paid the price for it." She picked up her helmet and tucked it under her arm. "I don't mean to sound callous, but he shouldn't have been trying to steal the formula for the Emmerson essencia."

With that, the Youngs set off toward the stairway.

"See you this evening at the Clear Creek Family Fest!" Sam tossed over his shoulder.

"Wow, Old Johnny knows how to fry a pie," said Owen, who had just crunched into his chocolate cream pie. "What flavor did you get, Alice?"

But Alice wasn't eating.

"Alice, what's wrong?" asked Franny.

Alice frowned. "So that confirms it. The Youngs did know Rupert had stolen the Emmerson's secret. How did they find that out?" She sighed. "I remember Suzie saying the essencia was to die for. But I wonder if she and Sam also thought it was worth killing for."

CHAPTER 9

"These *fun* honeymoon activities seem to be getting stranger and stranger," said Luke, opening the brochure he held, which gave a detailed account of the history and splendor of the World's Largest Walnut.

"What do you mean?" said Owen, looking up at the gargantuan nut, which stood eleven feet high. "This thing is epic!"

"Yeah, it's nuts," added Alice, rolling her eyes.

"Good one, Alice," said Ben with a snicker.

Alice and Luke had already posed for photos which

featured them pointing at the walnut with amazed expressions on their faces.

"So let's go over what we know so far about the case," said Luke. "It's not that I don't have confidence in Detective Mullins and his crew. But I just want to keep a finger on the pulse of this thing."

"So far, we have four suspects in mind," said Ben.

"That's right," said Franny. "Helena, because Rupert took advantage of her and broke her heart."

"And her brother, Max, because he loves his sister and was none too happy that Rupert tried to steal the family's secret formula," said Own.

"And finally, it could have been one of the Youngs," said Luke. "They came to the vineyard to learn about winemaking."

"And Suzie said they need something spectacular to make it in the business," added Alice. She paused thoughtfully. "And what about the Waxing Moon Winery?" she wondered. "They're probably tired of always coming in third around here. A special wine like the essencia could put them ahead if they knew how to make it."

"And after all, the dead man worked for Waxing Moon," said Luke, nodding. "Makes sense that it could've been them who sent him out as a spy."

"I'm calling Phillipa," said Alice, taking out her phone.

"The Waxing Moon manager lady? Wait—what good would that do?" asked Owen. "If she knew about a plan to steal the formula, she certainly wouldn't tell you."

"Don't worry," said Alice, dialing. "I have an idea about how to approach this. I'll put her on speaker phone. We have plenty of privacy—since, shockingly, we're the only people who ventured out to see the World's Largest Walnut today."

Phillipa picked up right away. "Hi Alice! Good to hear from you."

"Hi, Phillipa! You'll never believe where Luke and I are today."

Phillipa laughed. "Give me a hint," she said.

"Okay, let's see . . . It's rich in antioxidants and omega-3s . . ."

"Oy. You're at the World's Largest Walnut?"

"Yep. It's *Fabulous Bride*'s latest activity. And we zip lined this morning."

"Old Johnny's?"

"Yep."

"Bless you."

"Thank you. After this we have a stroll through the vineyard and then we're off to Oma's Candy Kitchen."

"Excellent fudge," said Phillipa. "Are you going to the Family Fest this evening at Clear Creek Cellars?"

"We'll be there," said Alice.

"Good. That event's actually a lot of fun."

"Glad to hear it." Alice paused for a beat. "Phillipa, I have a question."

"Sure. Shoot."

"Luke and I truly fell in love with that essencia at the wine tasting the other day."

"Don't blame you. It's amazing."

"But so expensive. We were wondering if Waxing Moon makes something similar—you know, like your own version of it."

"Don't I wish? Wine like that makes a vineyard famous. If we could make an essencia of our own?" She whistled. "That'd be good for business."

Everyone's eyes grew wide at this remark. Luke nodded at Alice to go on.

"Well, why don't you? I mean, why not make your own?"

"Great question. But to make an essencia, you have to be able to grow the right kind of grapes, and you have to have optimal conditions for the noble rot. Waxing Moon is just enough higher in elevation to be dryer, so the right rot could never happen here. We also have a different soil composition. There's less clay in the soil up here. We can't really grow the right kind of grapes even if we could get the right kind of rot." She chuckled.

"Oh." Alice looked at Luke. "So it's not even on the agenda there—to create an essencia?"

"No, that'd be a big waste of effort," said Phillipa.

"But we are developing a sweet red that we're hoping will make a good dessert wine. We're putting all of our resources into that now. Don't spread that around, by the way. It's not exactly a secret, but we aren't ready to formally announce it yet. It's going to be a few more years before we have a good bottle."

"How exciting!" said Alice. "You have my word, I won't tell a soul." She sighed. "Well, I guess Luke and I will have to chalk our essencia-tasting up as a once-in-a-lifetime experience."

Phillipa laughed. "I recommend you try a few different dessert wines. There are some very nice ones available at reasonable prices. I'll text you a few recommendations."

"Thanks, Phillipa," said Alice. "That sounds great."

They said their goodbyes and Alice hung up.

"Well, unless your friend Phillipa is an extremely good actress, Rupert wasn't spying on Waxing Moon's behalf when he stole that formula," said Owen. "Sounds like it's wouldn't be feasible for them to even attempt an essencia."

"But it's not like Rupert owned his own vineyard

either," said Alice. "I mean, it's not as though he planned to manufacture the wine himself." She thought for a moment. "No, I feel certain he was working for someone."

"Maybe the Youngs hired him—and then killed him once he'd told them the formula," said Ben. "After all, they wouldn't want that formula to fall into anyone else's hands, and Rupert probably had it memorized."

"You know what makes even more sense?" said Alice. "Clear Creek Cellars. They're the Emmersons' biggest rival. Maybe they hired Rupert to steal the formula."

"That makes sense," said Luke. "Those two vineyards have a long history."

Alice nodded. "And not a pretty one."

CHAPTER 10

"So, basically, we have two sets of suspects," said Alice as they all took an afternoon stroll through the vineyard. "First, we have the Sloans at Waxing Moon and the Youngs. All of them might be willing to kill for the essencia formula."

"Right," said Owen. "And second, we have Helena and Max Emmerson. Either of them might kill to *protect* the formula—and stop Rupert from spilling the grapes, so to speak."

"Hey—while we're out here, let's walk over to where you saw the shooting happen, Alice," said Luke. "We can go over the area one more time, just in case Detective Mullens missed something."

"Good idea," said Alice. "It's not far from here." She led the group down one long pathway that ran between two sets of vines, then turned right and went further down, finally coming to a stop and looking around, confused. "This place is huge. It's way too easy to get turned around."

"Let's get reoriented," said Luke. "The inn is that way." He pointed to the right of where they were standing. "The balloon took off and landed in the field next to it, so we were drifting in that direction from . . . that way. Little Bavaria is southwest of here."

"Gosh I love a man with a sense of direction," said Alice.

"So basically, this was our path across the sky," said Luke, motioning in an arc above them.

"I remember seeing a huge stone . . ." Alice walked a bit further. When she got to the end of one row of vines and looked further down the pathway, she spotted the large stone—the same one she'd managed to find when they'd come running this way after landing. "Come on!" she said, picking up her pace and jogging toward the stone.

Everyone followed until they all arrived next to it. Then Alice led them down the row of vines where she'd seen the shooting. They all walked up and down that row and those around it, but found no sign of anything amiss.

"Nothing but deer poop," said Alice with a disappointed sigh.

"Unless this is the wrong rock," Owen called from where he was standing, on top of the stone. "Didn't you say it was sort of gusty toward the end of the balloon ride? And wouldn't that have meant you could've been blown off course?"

"But this *was* the stone. I'm sure of it," said Alice as she scrambled up and joined Owen. "Oh. Hold on. Maybe this *wasn't* the stone." From that vantage point, Alice could see several other stones of similar size in the vicinity.

"And didn't the detective say they found the body back in the trees?" asked Franny, who had hopped up onto the stone with ease.

"What are you? Some kind of mountain goat?" said Owen.

"Look! There's a big stone way over that way, near the tree line," said Franny, pointing.

They all ran over to that stone and down the rows of vines near it.

"And here we are," said Owen, pointing at the ground between two rows. "X marks the spot."

"Blood," said Luke, squatting down. "Good eyes, Owen." He stood. "We need to go over this area with a fine-toothed comb. Look for any little clue that might've escaped notice in the excitement of finding the body yesterday."

They all spent the next quarter hour scouring the area for clues. Ben and Luke found where Rupert's body had been dragged through the grass. Alice felt her stomach lurch when they found the area in the trees where a quick grave had been dug.

Then she caught sight of something glittering in the afternoon sunlight between the rows of grapes a short distance from where they'd found the blood. "What's that?" She went to where the shiny object lay and bent down to pick it up. "Hey, I recognize this," she said.

"Wow. That's gorgeous," said Owen, leaning in to see. "Looks familiar."

"That's because you've seen it about a thousand times since arriving here," said Alice as Franny joined them. "It's the Emmerson family crest. All the Emmersons wear this."

"It's totally bejeweled!" said Owen, taking the glittering pendant and turning it over in his hands. "Are those rubies?"

"They wear them every day," said Alice. "And Suzie told me only the family and very important staff members have them."

By that time, Ben and Luke had joined them, and they all stood around in a circle, looking at the pendant.

"So, say there was a scuffle between Rupert and his killer . . ." said Owen.

"This got torn off and left behind," said Alice, nodding. "And the killer noticed it missing, but hasn't been able to find it."

"And only two people from our suspect list could possibly own that pendant," said Franny. "Helena and Max Emmerson."

"What we know for sure," said Luke, "is that this little jewel puts its owner at the site of a murder. We need to go find out who this belongs to."

"Here. I have a tissue in my pocket," said Alice, taking the pendant from Owen and wrapping it up carefully.

They all walked back up to the inn, but as they passed the barn, they noticed a photoshoot going on that, for once, had nothing to do with *Fabulous Bride Magazine*. It appeared to be a shoot for the vineyard. Helena was standing at the entrance to the barn, hair gleaming and makeup carefully applied, holding a bottle of the Emmerson Family Merlot and smiling at the camera.

"Let's get closer," whispered Alice. "We can see if she's wearing the crest."

They all casually strolled in that direction, and moved in near enough to see the details of Helena's outfit.

"Hey, folks, be sure to stay over this way," said Max, stepping out from behind a screen that had been set up for light control. "But you're welcome to stay and watch the shoot. We're creating a new ad campaign and updating our website."

Alice tried to stay calm as she noticed that Max's pendant was missing from its usual place on his lapel. She looked at Owen and Franny to see if they'd noticed too. Owen gave a microscopic nod.

"Thanks, Mr. Emmerson," Alice said.

"Please. Call me Max."

Alice nodded. "Thanks, Max."

They all moved over a bit and watched as the photographer snapped his shots, occasionally switching out the bottle of wine Helena was holding or adjusting her stance. Helena was clearly wearing her pendant. It sparkled beautifully in the sunlight.

"So, that settles that," Owen whispered. "We've got motive and now we can place Max at the scene of the crime."

"We need to take the pendant to the police," whispered Luke. "It'll be up to them to take the next steps."

Just then, the photoshoot ended, and Helena set down the bottle of Chardonnay she was holding and stretched her arms.

"We got plenty of great shots, Mr. Emmerson," the photographer assured Max. "I'm going to head out into the vines and get a few closeups of the grapes and scenery. Then I'll take a few inside the barn and inn."

"Sounds great," said Max, shaking the photographer's hand. He walked over to his sister. "Good job, Helena."

"My arms are so tired," she complained.

"Poor thing," he teased. "Having to hold up all those bottles of wine and look pretty. How do you endure it?" He gave her a playful jab. "Now give me back my pin."

Helena rolled her eyes and took off the jeweled crest.

"I can't believe you lost yours," said Max, pinning the crest to his lapel. "Shame on you, little sis'. These things aren't cheap."

Helena reddened. "I'm sure it'll turn up. Or I'll order a new one."

Max snickered and walked off after the photographer.

"So, Helena's the killer," whispered Owen. "A woman scorned."

"I don't know . . ." said Franny.

"Something in my gut doesn't feel right about it either, Franny," said Alice. She walked over to Helena.

"Alice, what are you—" Luke said after her. But it was too late. Alice had already taken the jeweled pendant out of her pocket and unwrapped it.

"Helena, I think I found something of yours," said Alice.

Helena's eyes grew huge when she saw the pendant. "Where did—how—"

"It was out in the vineyard," said Alice, nodding back in the direction they'd come from.

"Thank you so much," said Helena, composing herself and reaching for the pendant, which Alice quickly pulled away.

"Not so fast," she said. "First, I'd love to hear how this ended up out there among the vines."

Tears quickly filled Helena's eyes, and her face fell.

"You mean, you're wondering why you found it around the same place where you saw Rupert get . . ."

"Killed," Alice finished. "Yes, that question had crossed my mind."

Helena met Alice's eyes. "Because I gave that to him," she said, her voice cracking. She cleared her throat. "I gifted that to him as a symbol of my commitment to him." She stopped and cleared her throat again. "I'm *not* going to cry over that man anymore." She took a step closer to Alice and started to say something else, then glanced at the rest of the group, who were not-so-subtly listening in.

"You hold it together, sister," said Owen, giving Helena an encouraging thumbs up. "You deserve better than that old Rupert."

Helena gave Owen a grateful smile.

"You were saying?" said Alice, looking back at Helena.

"He'd asked me to marry him," said Helena. "He hinted that he wanted to be part of this place—part of the Emmerson family. That he wanted to help us continue in the business of making unique wines,

cultivating the business like we cultivate our grapes."
She flung a hand toward the vineyards that stretched
out behind Alice. "I gave him that crest as my way of
saying, 'Hey Rupert, welcome to the family.' How
stupid was that?"

Alice sighed and laid a hand on Helena's arm.
"People do crazy things for love, you know. And how
can anyone fault you for trusting the man you loved?"

"Love." Helena scoffed. "He was just using me to get
the family formula for our essencia." She looked at
the group. "I know it sounds juvenile. Secret formulas. Spies. It's just wine, after all. But our family has
guarded that formula for three generations. Of course
it would be *me* that had it romanced right out from
under her!"

"Helena, you're being too hard on yourself—" Franny
started to say.

"And what's worse is, the police are going to think I
killed Rupert. Especially now that you found *that*
right where he died." Helena groaned. "It's like he's
haunting me from the grave!"

"So, you were there? In the vineyard? Just before he
was murdered?" asked Alice.

Helena nodded. "That's why I was asking you where you thought you saw the person get shot," she said. "That spot in the vineyard—near the big rock and the woods? That's our usual meeting place. *Was* our usual meeting place. We'd had a huge argument. I was starting to suspect what he was really after. I confronted him about it. Told him to give me back my pendant. But he wouldn't. He said he loved me and that I was just being paranoid, that he'd never betray me or my family. And I fell for it! I left him standing there, and the next thing I hear, someone's out there, shot to death. When the police came that first time, and I saw them going out into the vines, I had a terrible foreboding feeling in my gut that it was Rupert. And then I was so relieved when they didn't find a body. But I couldn't shake the feeling that something terrible had happened. And it had!"

"You were the one who called the police to come back here," said Alice.

"Yes," said Helena, wiping her eyes. "But I did it anonymously because I knew that if Rupert really was dead . . . I was probably the next to last person to have seen him. And we'd just argued. And what if someone saw me or heard us yelling at each other? I'd be the prime suspect."

"And now you're grieving the loss of someone you loved, and you can't really even talk about it," said Alice, noticing that Helena suddenly looked extremely young. "This is all too much, huh?"

Helena nodded, wiping her eyes again.

"It's okay to cry," said Owen, putting an arm around her. "You just go ahead and let it all out."

"And it's okay to grieve, even though Rupert was a jerk to you," added Alice. "I'm so sorry for your loss."

"Thank you," said Helena, tears rolling down her cheeks. Then she looked hopefully at Alice and Luke. "Please. If you remember anything you saw from the balloon—if you recall any detail about the person who shot Rupert—*please* let the police know."

"We will," said Alice, and she handed the Emmerson crest to Helena.

CHAPTER 11

Four o'clock Sunday afternoon meant that Alice and Luke were due at Oma's Candy Kitchen in downtown Little Bavaria. "Oma," whose actual name turned out to be Hannah Schmidt, greeted them wearing a traditional German dirndl dress, her long gray hair done up in braids that formed a band around her head. She was actually quite lovely—not the pink-cheeked, plump little lady Alice had imagined she'd be. No, Oma was a bundle of energy, with the heart of a candy maker, and the shrewd mind of a businesswoman.

"You're right on time," she said, glancing at her watch and smiling at Luke and Alice. "The *Fabulous*

Bride photographer is all set up, and I have an array of goodies for you to sample."

"Wonderful!" said Alice. "We've brought a few friends along. They're all candy enthusiasts and will do some shopping while we're taking the photos."

Hannah smiled at Owen, Franny, and Ben. "Make yourselves at home. If you see something you'd like to try, just ask me. I'm always happy to offer samples. We have every treat you can imagine, from handmade hard candies to licorice to gourmet chocolates and caramels. Enjoy!"

Alice and Luke got to sample Oma's vast selection of bonbons—with colorful, glossy coats of chocolate, and melting fillings in flavors like Bavarian Cream, Italian Chestnut, Vanilla Coffee, and Amaretto Delight. They ended up buying a large box of the confections to take back to the inn, and Owen, Ben, and Franny walked out of Oma's with bags full of treats as well.

"It's official. I love Oma," said Owen as they walked down the quaint village's main street—aptly called *Hauptstrasse*. "I never knew there was such a thing as a honey lavender bonbon."

"I like the gourmet gumdrops," said Franny, popping one of the little sugary treats into her mouth. "Mmm. Toasted marshmallow. Who ever heard of a toasted marshmallow *gumdrop*?"

"Where are we headed next?" asked Ben.

"To Clear Creek Cellars," said Alice. "They're hosting a Family Fest there this evening. We should be able to walk there from here."

"Wow," said Owen. "Children and wine. What an interesting concept."

"There will apparently be all kinds of family-friendly events," said Alice.

"And most parents could do with an evening glass of wine, let me tell you," said Franny, laughing.

"So, we'll be seeing several of the people from our suspect list," said Luke. "Suzie and Sam said they'll be there."

"Yep," said Alice. "Not to mention the Sloan family. The vineyard was founded by Elizabeth Emmerson-Sloan and her husband, Oliver. Their children and their spouses ran it next, and now, much of the operation has fallen into the hands of Elizabeth and Oliver's grandson, Forrest—although his parents and a few cousins are still involved in the business too. But apparently Forrest has taken a very good vineyard and is working toward making it great."

"I know about him," said Owen. "He was featured in one of my chef magazines a few months ago. He's quite the looker."

"Suzie was totally starstruck when we saw him at the wine tasting," said Alice, nodding.

They walked along a bit further, admiring the Bavarian architecture of the town.

"It's like we're in some kind of Alpine wonderland," said Owen.

"I know," said Alice. "I can't get over it. I feel like we're in Europe."

"Old World Europe," agreed Luke. "Look at the red tile roofs."

"And the scrolling around the windows. And the overflowing flower boxes around every little balcony," said Alice.

"Even the lampposts are adorable," said Franny.

"And the air smells amazing," said Owen. "I can smell sausage and potatoes and chocolate and bread."

"The four food groups!" said Ben.

They followed Alice's *Visitors' Guide to Little Bavaria*, winding their way through the downtown, then along quiet neighborhood streets, and finally to a gorgeous country road that led to Clear Creek Cellars, which lay just at the edge of town.

"Wow," said Alice, looking out over the vineyard and across the gently rolling mountains. "I can see why Elizabeth and Oscar picked this spot. It's gorgeous!"

They walked down the winding brick driveway toward the charming main building, which sat in a beam of sunlight, surrounded by colorful spring flowers and trees.

"Alice! Luke! Climb aboard!"

Alice looked ahead to see a large wagon filled with bales of hay, pulled by two huge horses, just emerging from around the back side of the building. The Youngs were sitting on one of the bales, waving furiously.

"Let's go," said Alice, picking up her pace.

"They could be killers," said Owen under his breath. "But okay." He turned to Franny. "I like going on hay rides with murderer suspects. Don't you?"

The driver slowed the horses, and everyone clambered up into the wagon.

"Perfect timing," said Suzie. "We're taking a tour of the place. This hayride will cover the vineyard and the cellar. We're actually going to get to walk through the barrel room!"

"And Forrest Sloan himself is going to talk about the hallmark wines of this region," added Sam.

"Perfect!" said Alice, nudging Luke.

The horse-drawn wagon meandered through the vineyard, the guide explaining about the varieties of grapes and the richness of the soil and pointing out the cottage where Elizabeth and Oliver had lived when they'd first settled on this piece of land. When they came to the buildings, they were shown where the offices and gift shop were, along with the tasting room and the production area. They talked about presses, pumps, tanks, and barrels. They disembarked from the hayride and met Forrest Sloan, who walked them along through rows of tanks and barrels, talking about the different kinds of wood used to age the wines and which barrel contained what.

Alice inhaled deeply, savoring the scents of oak and grapes and time. She thought that if *waiting* had a smell, this would be it—waiting for something wonderful to happen.

After Forrest concluded his talk, the visitors were encouraged to look around on their own for a bit before the hayride headed back to the tasting room and gift shop.

"Here's our chance to talk to Forrest," whispered Franny.

"As soon as the Youngs are done talking to him," Alice whispered back.

The group as a whole wandered over near to where Forrest stood talking to the Youngs, but were careful not to appear to be eavesdropping. But the room was fairly quiet, and it wasn't hard to hear snatches of conversation. The Youngs were asking lots of questions. Forrest politely commented on their obvious passion for winemaking, and they excitedly told him about the land they'd purchased and their plans to start their own vineyard.

Suzie lowered her voice just a bit when she asked Forrest about a trio of particular grapes they were interested in cultivating. Alice couldn't make out every word, but she definitely heard "Yellow Muscat."

"That's one of the three grapes used to make essencia!" said Alice. "George told us about it when we were up in the balloon."

"So the Youngs might be thinking about creating their own essencia," said Luke.

"Which would mean they'd be very interested to know how the *only* Tennessee essencia is formulated," said Alice.

"Forrest is starting to look a bit hot under the collar," said Owen. "Look at him. No! Not all at once!"

"He's turning purple!" whispered Franny.

"He doesn't like the line of questioning coming from the Youngs," said Luke. "Look at his body language."

"Not all at once!" Owen said again. "*One* of us can look. Everyone else keep acting like we're fascinated by this barrel here. Ben, you look."

Ben glanced in the direction of the threesome, then looked down and nodded. "Oh, his body language has changed since that conversation began," he said. "Forrest's arms are crossed. He's red in the face. He keeps looking around like he wants to get away."

Forrest suddenly said, in a loud and irritated voice, "If you will excuse me," and stalked out of the room. The Youngs looked after him in stunned silence for a moment, then walked toward the exit themselves. As they passed, Alice heard Suzie muttering to Sam, "It better have been worth the risk. Everything's riding on this."

As soon as they'd left the building, the group reviewed what they'd heard.

"So, much for feeling out Forrest," said Alice. "Who knows where he went after storming off."

"But wow," said Owen. "The Youngs are looking all too suspicious. What do you think Suzie meant about it being *worth the risk*?"

"Exactly what I'm wondering," said Luke. "Could she mean they took a risk in killing Rupert?"

"We don't have time to ponder that now," said Alice,

taking Luke's hand. "We're due over at the Family Fun Rock Climbing Wall Competition. We're getting our photo taken climbing the wall together."

"Oh, boy," said Owen. "Does the winner get a trophy?"

"I think so," said Alice.

"And Franny's still on her competitive streak . . ." said Owen.

"I love rock climbing walls!" said Franny.

"Stand back, everyone. She's on the rampage!" said Owen.

CHAPTER 12

Franny smiled at the camera as Forrest Sloan presented her with her *Champion Adult Rock Climber* trophy—a small brass tower with a large, actual rock glued to the top.

"Could you believe the way she attacked that wall?" Owen said as the gathered crowd applauded. "It was like she was possessed!"

"I've never seen anything like it," said Ben, shaking his head. "My wife, the rock climbing champ. I'm so proud of her."

Franny jogged over and joined them. "Wow, that was fun!" She sniffed the air. "Mmm. Someone's fired up the grill. All that climbing made me hungry."

"Good, because it's time for the dinner portion of Clear Creek's Family Fest." Alice glanced at her schedule. "And it's called *Kebab Fest*. They sure do like fests around here."

"Makes me homesick for Blue Valley," said Owen. And he was right. Blue Valley was a festival town.

"Me too," said Alice. "But the beauty of being here is that I'm not the one in charge of the event."

"That's right," said Luke, putting an arm around Alice. "You can just relax and enjoy yourself."

"And nab the killer," added Owen.

"Well, yeah. There's that, too," said Luke. "Let's go see about those kebabs. Franny's right. It smells amazing."

They followed their noses—and the rest of the fest-goers—to a wide, open grassy area, where wooden tables were scattered about, along with large baskets filled with picnic blankets. Families were choosing tables and spreading blankets and helping themselves to glasses of fresh lemonade or wine. A long table was being filled with good things as they came off the grill. There were fun hot dog and French fry kebabs with mini ears of corn for the kids; and kebabs laden with everything from juicy steak to buttery shrimp and colorful vegetables for the adults. A second table was heaped with dessert kebabs—skewers of cubed cakes, candies, chocolate-dipped berries and a selection of sauces and frostings to dip them in. Alice and Luke posed for the magazine, feeding each other and laughing while holding their kebabs, and then everyone settled in to enjoy the feast. Owen spread a huge blanket out for them and Franny and Ben brought glasses and a bottle of beautiful pink Clear Creek Rosé.

Alice saw the Youngs choosing a picnic blanket from one of the baskets.

"Suzie! Sam! Come sit over here!" she called, waving at them.

"Good thinking, Alice," whispered Owen. "We can find out what all that talk earlier in the barrel room was about."

"Because something they said definitely made Forrest very angry," said Franny.

Luke chuckled and nudged Ben. "It's kind of fun to see their crime-solving process up close, isn't it?"

"From the inside," agreed Ben.

Usually, back in Blue Valley when a crime happened, Ben and Luke got busy investigating in the official way—as police captain and head detective. So they never really saw firsthand how Alice, Owen, and Franny worked a case—oftentimes using their own unique, sometimes downright strange, methods.

Sam and Suzie spread their blanket, got their food, and finally came and sat down.

"You two look glum—and you *never* look glum," Alice said, noting the troubled looks on their faces. "Everything okay?"

Suzie looked at Sam, whose eyes glistened with tears. "Don't cry, Sam. It'll all work out," she said, pressing Sam's hand with her own. Then she turned to Alice. "He's the most sensitive man in the world, and it just breaks my heart when he's sad."

"Is there anything we can do?" asked Alice, smiling gently. "I mean, why are you sad?"

"I'm surprised you didn't hear Forrest Sloan's little tirade earlier in the barrel room," said Suzie.

Sam sniffled. "I mean, I get that he didn't want to talk

to us about making an essencia, but did he have to be so rude about it?"

Alice looked from Sam to Suzie. "But what would Forrest know about essencias? Clear Creek doesn't make that wine, do they?"

"But everyone knows they'd like to," said Suzie. "They've tried through the years—ever since Elizabeth Emmerson-Sloan came up with the idea."

"We overstepped . . . we shouldn't have asked him about that," said Sam, looking at his wife. "It's a sore subject around here."

"So you want to formulate an essencia at your own vineyard?" Owen asked.

Suzie looked ashamed. "We did," she finally said. "And we—well, we let things get out of hand on that quest. The thing is, our land is at the right altitude. We have the right soil, the right climate . . ."

"But we don't have eight years to turn a profit," said Sam. "It just takes too long. And we still don't know the exact ingredients or the secrets to the fermentation process."

Alice nodded. "I imagine there are people who would

do just about anything to lay their hands on those secrets."

That was when Suzie burst into tears. "Oh, Alice! We *were* those people!"

"Confession alert!" Owen whispered into Alice's ear.

"What do you mean?" asked Alice, elbowing Owen.

They all leaned forward just a hair, waiting for Suzie's response.

"We might as well tell all," said Sam. "We came on this trip to learn the secrets of the essencia." He bit his lower lip. "We're not even really newlyweds!"

There was a collective gasp from the group.

"It's true!" said Suzie. "We've been married for five years. We had to say we were newlyweds to get the honeymoon package discount. Emmerson is the only vineyard in the state that makes an essencia, and we were determined to crack that code. Oh, how foolish we were!" she wailed.

"So what did you do?" asked Alice. "I mean, did you get any information at all?"

"We snooped around a little," said Suzie with a nod.

"But then we stumbled upon that Rupert Billings, talking on the phone about the formula and how he'd managed to steal it."

"It really was a bizarre coincidence," said Sam. "And it's all because there's no phone reception at the Emmerson Estate. We were headed to that little rise to call home to check on our daughter—she's with Suzie's parents for the week."

"She's three," said Suzie.

"So, we were walking over to make the call on Thursday evening."

"It was after dark," added Suzie. "We call every night to say goodnight."

"Anyway," Sam went on, "Rupert was already at the rise, but his back was turned to us, so he didn't see us walking up. He was talking in a hushed voice, but we got an earful anyway. He was telling someone that he'd stolen the formula for the Emmersons' essencia."

"He told them he'd meet them Friday evening around sunset, at the usual meeting place out in the vineyard," said Suzie. "Gosh, I'm so ashamed of this now. We canceled our hot air balloon ride and waited around until we saw Rupert, sneaking out among the rows of vines. We almost didn't recognize him, because he was wearing an Emmerson uniform, and as you know, he worked at Waxing Moon as their sommelier. We saw him well before sunset, going out to the vineyard. We waited a while, then snuck out there ourselves. We saw Helena Emmerson walking back toward the inn, but luckily, she was too upset to notice us."

"Was she with Rupert?" asked Alice, trying to keep her voice even and calm.

"It looked like she had been," said Suzie. "She was walking out of the vineyard at breakneck speed, looking very worried. We hid behind a bush like two evil spies. I still can't believe we did it!"

"Then what happened?" asked Franny.

Alice looked and saw that the whole group was listening with rapt attention now, kebabs frozen in mid-air.

"We found where Rupert was, toward the back of the vineyard," said Sam. "He was talking to some guy we couldn't see. Rupert talked about the grapes used for the essencia, then he said he had the formula and process memorized, thanks to Helena trusting him. But he said he wasn't willing to share it unless he got more money."

"That was when the other person started to express doubt that Rupert had actually gotten the real formula," said Suzie. "And then Rupert said, 'Here's proof,' and held out the Emmerson crest."

"Helena's missing pendant," said Owen.

"And then the other guy grabbed the crest and threw it on the ground," said Sam. "Can you believe that?"

"That made Rupert *furious*," said Suzie. "The other guy took out his wallet and said, 'What's this going to cost me?' and Rupert yelled, 'Too late now!' and grabbed the wallet and threw it far off into the trees. I mean, that thing must've flown a mile! Rupert could've been a great quarterback."

"At that point, could you see the person Rupert was talking to?" asked Luke.

"No. We never did," Sam said, shaking his head sadly. "You could cut the sense of danger with a knife at that point."

"We knew we were in over our heads," said Suzie.

"So what did you do?" asked Ben.

"We snuck back a few yards, then ran like the wind back to the inn. Next thing we know, Rupert's being carried away in a body bag," said Sam.

"We never saw the other guy's face, but we know it was a man, based on his voice," said Suzie. "Do you think the person Rupert was talking to was the killer?"

"Well, of course there's a very good chance of that," said Luke. "But since you didn't actually see him pull a gun or anything, we can't be certain. Someone else could've come out after that . . ."

"Did you happen to look up and see us in a balloon?" asked Alice. "Because I never saw the two of you down on the ground."

"We didn't see you," said Suzie, shaking her head. "But we were pretty focused on what was happening on the ground."

"We were incredibly stupid," said Sam. "To think, we put ourselves in that kind of danger—all over *wine*." He looked at Suzie and took her hand. "And you know what? We don't need to steal anyone else's formulas anyway. We'll come up with our own brilliant wines. We never should've thought otherwise."

Suzie leaned over and kissed her husband. "You're absolutely right."

After that, everyone enjoyed the meal and the sunset. A few hours later, they climbed into their shuttle back to the Emmerson Estate. The Youngs, who had driven over in their own car, waved goodbye and drove out of the parking lot ahead of them.

"So it wasn't the Youngs," said Owen, taking his seat.

"Nope, doesn't look like it," said Alice.

"My money's on Forrest Sloan or Maximilian Emmerson," said Franny.

"You know what I can't stop thinking about?" said Alice, looking out the window as the shuttle moved down the road. "That flying wallet."

CHAPTER 13

"Think about it," said Alice as they disembarked from the shuttle back at the Emmerson Estate. "Rupert flung the killer's wallet into the trees. Would the guy really have taken the time to go look for it—between shooting Rupert and burying him and running away before we got to the area? I mean, I know Luke, George, and I ran to the wrong set of vines, but we were within earshot of where they found Rupert's body. Surely he didn't hang around to look for his wallet for too long."

"So maybe it's still there," said Owen, looking out over the vines.

"We need to go look," said Franny.

"But it's already dark," said Ben. "We're unlikely to find anything tonight."

"I agree," said Luke. "Maybe we should go out and check in the morning."

"And give the killer time to sneak out there and find it before we do?" said Alice. "I think not. Owen, show them your flashlight."

"The flashlight on your phone?" asked Ben, curiously looking over Owen's shoulder as he took out his phone.

"Yes," said Owen. "But not the flashlight that came with the phone. This," he said snapping on a blinding white light, "is my Super-Bright Wilderness Emergency Signal app." He cast the light around, illuminating the darkness. "Three bucks."

"Impressive," said Luke.

They ventured into the vines, now knowing exactly where they needed to go. They passed over the cell phone-reception rise, along the gravel path that ran between two different varieties of grapes, past the first giant rock—which Owen had dubbed "The

Wrong Rock," and toward the sets of vines that bumped up against the tree line.

"Owen! Douse the light! Fast!" said Luke, putting a hand on Owen's shoulder. "Did you hear that?" he whispered.

Everyone froze. Voices could be heard up ahead in the distance.

"Someone's very angry from the sound of it," said Franny.

"And if my guess is right, they're arguing right around the scene of the crime," said Luke.

"For crying out loud! Can't these people pick a new meeting place?" whispered Owen.

"Let's get closer. But be careful," warned Luke.

They all moved together in one clump. Owen had linked arms with Alice and Franny.

"I don't like this," Alice whispered. "A chill just ran up and down my spine."

"Maybe we should call the police," said Ben.

"There's no reception here," said Luke. "And by the

time we get back to the rise, someone could be in trouble. Let's go a little further and see if there's any actual danger."

They came to a row of tall bushes that separated one grouping of vines from another and ducked into the bushes. From there, they could see the two men standing in the moonlight.

"Forrest Sloan!" whispered Alice.

"And Maximillian Emmerson," said Luke. "Listen. They're talking about Rupert."

"I never should have trusted that idiot, Billings!" said Forrest. "He seemed so smart—so certain he could get us what is rightfully ours."

"Is that why you called me out here—to come and insult me on my own estate?" said Max.

"If I'd asked you to come over to Clear Creek, would you have?" There was a pause. "Yeah. I thought not," said Forrest. "Because everyone knows you Emmersons are too good for everyone else." He laughed, sounding slightly delirious. "Good thing your stupid sister was so gullible! She fell for Rupert like a ton of bricks. What a loser."

Max shoved Forrest, who fell back, but hopped right up.

"Don't you *ever* talk about my sister! Now I want you off our land. You're obviously drunk!"

"First, the essencia was my grandmother's idea. Second, I paid Rupert handsomely to steal it. The jerk had it memorized and demanded more money. He got what he deserved as far as I'm concerned. But now I'm here to claim what's mine!" His words were starting to slur a little bit.

"No, Forrest. And it's time you learned you can't *buy* your way to a great wine. Everything's not for sale. And so what if your grandmother wanted to make an essencia? Lots of people do! Only a true winemaker can formulate something unforgettable. Just let it go."

"I won't let it go! And you and your stupid sister can kiss your success goodbye!" Forrest rushed at Max, who mentioned something about leaving Helena out of it and then took a swing at Forrest but missed. Then Forrest ran off toward the wooded tree line, and Max made to go after him.

"Get back here now, Forrest! I want you gone!"

"He's going to get himself killed," said Luke, leading the group out of the bushes. "Time to step in and lend a hand."

"What are you all doing here?" asked Max, shocked to see them.

"We're here to help," said Luke. "But first, do you have your wallet on you?"

Max frowned and patted his jacket pockets. "Sure," he said, taking out his wallet and holding it up. "Why?"

"Just making sure," said Luke, nodding at Alice, who nodded back. "Ben, let's go. You three, call the police."

Ben and Luke ran off at top speed toward the woods.

CHAPTER 14

"I'll call the police!" said Franny, running off in the direction of the cell phone-reception rise.

"I'm so confused," said Max as they walked at a slower pace back toward the inn. "Were you all just out walking around in the dark?"

"We've been doing a little investigating," said Owen. "We hear about an unsolved crime and we just have to meddle." He shrugged modestly.

"Oh—so you've been looking into Rupert Billings's murder." Max nodded in understanding. "How good of you. How brave."

"Well, I was the one who saw Rupert get shot from

the hot air balloon," said Alice. "You can't see a thing like that happen and not want justice to be served."

"So you saw it all, huh?" asked Max. "What happened? I mean—other than the part where Rupert got shot?"

"Hard to say, really, except that he and Forrest were fighting, and then Forrest got up holding the gun. But Rupert never did."

Max nodded. "Must've been terrible, to see something like that. And here you are, on your honeymoon."

"It was," Alice admitted. "But it must be terrible for you, too, knowing that everyone wants to steal your family's secrets."

"Yes, I've had about enough of that," said Max. "I mean, just this week, we had Rupert and Forrest. And that other couple—the Youngs—they hinted at it, too."

"You know, I saw Forrest and Rupert talking outside the barn at the wine tasting," said Alice. "I told Luke then that they were having some kind of clandestine discussion."

"You have good instincts," said Max. "I wonder how long the two of them were in cahoots."

"Crazy!" said Owen. "That essencia must be some wine."

"Oh it is," said Max. "I'll break out a bottle when we get back to the inn. You can try it."

"That'd be amazing!" said Owen.

Alice suddenly stopped walking. "Max, how did you . . ." She looked closer at him for the first time that evening. Her heart began to pound when she noticed what Max was wearing. A dark sweat suit. A hooded jacket. "I mean, uh, you look like you're dressed to go out for a jog or something."

"I am," said Max, looking down at his clothes. "I love to run through the vineyard after dark, when the guests have all gone home or gone into the inn for the night. Clears my head." He paused, then looked at Alice.

Alice tried to steady her breathing. She could feel her face getting hot. "Sounds—"

"You know, don't you?" Max wasn't smiling anymore. "You figured it out."

"Figured what out?" asked Owen.

But Max didn't answer, and he didn't break eye contact with Alice for a second.

"How did you know the Youngs had tried to steal the formula?" Alice asked quietly.

"Let's walk a different direction," said Max, turning away from the inn and taking out a gun.

"What? It was *you*?" Owen's eyes grew large.

"You were probably hiding in the same bushes we hid in tonight," said Alice. "You saw the Youngs follow Rupert. You hid and watched Rupert's meeting with Forrest—probably ready to jump out the second Rupert started to rattle off the secret formula." She looked at Max. "But he never did, did he?"

Max shook his head slowly.

Alice went on. "Rupert wanted more money, Forrest made him mad, and Forrest left. By then, the Youngs had already scurried back to the inn. And that was when you saw your chance. The formula was in Rupert's memory—not written down. He would've sold it to the highest bidder, given the chance. But if you killed him, it would be secure."

"Correct," said Max. "Almost." He sighed. "I didn't confront Rupert for stealing the formula. I'm sick of that stupid formula! I confronted him because he hurt my sister." Max held out the gun. "This isn't—"

"Don't point that thing at—"

Owen's words were interrupted, for at that moment, time seemed to stand still as a battle cry was heard coming from the shadows a few steps away, and Franny appeared, running at top speed, her rock climbing trophy poised above her head. A split second later, the trophy had come squarely down onto Max's skull, and he'd fallen to the ground, where Franny—now with Owen and Alice's help—managed to pin Max's arms and legs down and take away his gun.

Just then Ben and Luke—a slightly more sober Forrest trying to keep up behind them—came running up. Franny quickly handed Ben the gun.

"You should have seen your wife, Ben," said Owen. "Turns out, she's a warrior banshee at heart."

Max let out a pained grown. "My head," he said.

"It broke my trophy," said Franny with a sniff. "That's some hard head you've got."

Sirens could be heard arriving at the inn, and Owen flipped on his bright light to signal the police where to come.

"Please, I beg you," Max said from where he still sat on the ground, rubbing his head. "Turn that insanely bright light off."

"Sorry, but I don't think I will," said Owen.

CHAPTER 15

"It's true. There's no place like home," said Owen as he, Alice, and Franny took their usual seats in their rooftop garden early in the evening a few days later.

"I'm so glad to be home," said Franny, snuggling nine-month-old Theo, who cooed happily in his mother's arms.

"We're all definitely going to need a rest after that vacation," said Alice.

Luke and Ben came through the French doors from Alice and Luke's living room.

"Let's eat," said Ben, holding up bags from the Smiling Hound, the pub across the street.

Alice sighed contentedly as she reached into a bag and pulled out a big basket of onion rings. "I never would've thought I'd say this after all of the wonderful food we ate on our honeymoon, but the Smiling Hound beats them all."

"Hands down," agreed Owen, stuffing an onion ring into his mouth while unwrapping his cheeseburger. "But the post-vacation detox *has* to start tomorrow," he added.

They all settled in around the café table with their food, collectively feeling glad to be home as they watched the sun begin to sink behind the tops of the Smoky Mountains that surrounded their little town.

"So, is Max going to be in jail for quite some time?" asked Franny.

"Actually, I have some news on that front," said Luke. "I just had a call from Detective Mullins. We followed up on the case, detective to detective, and it seems Max's story checked out. He'd been out for his evening jog when he saw the Youngs sneaking out into the vineyard in the dark, following Rupert. He decided to see what was going on. After the Youngs ran back to the inn, Max did confront Rupert, in part because he was angry that Rupert had stolen the Emmersons' formula, of course, but even more so because he'd insulted and hurt Helena. He and Rupert got into a shoving match, Rupert pulled a gun, and as Max was wrestling it away from him, it went off, killing Rupert. Max never meant for it to happen— and the gun was definitely registered to Rupert. But Max was afraid of what would happen to him when the police found out. He knew he had several strong motives to have murdered Rupert and that it wouldn't look good if he fessed up. So in the heat of the moment, he tried to cover the whole thing up."

"And then later, of course, he realized that if he was found out, he'd look even guiltier because of that," added Ben.

"So, he didn't say anything," said Alice. "And hoped it would all just go away."

"Yep," said Luke. "He took the gun, stashed the body, and ran away."

"And when he pulled the gun on us in the vineyard, he wasn't planning to shoot us with it, was he?" Alice guessed.

"It wasn't even loaded," said Luke. "He said he was

out walking the vineyard when Forrest called him and demanded to talk to him. Max had been trying to clear his head, considering whether he should throw the gun into the lake. When you'd obviously figured out the truth, Alice, he panicked again, took the gun out, and was hoping you'd run away and he could run the other direction and toss it into the lake."

"He definitely isn't the best under pressure," said Owen with a chuckle. "He wasn't even holding it right."

"I guess the secret to the Emmersons' essencia is safe and sound," said Alice ruefully. "Rupert had memorized it, but now he's dead." She paused. "But you know what I keep thinking about? The fact that Max and Forrest are cousins. First cousins! Isn't it a shame they can't work together and get over the past?"

"Good news there, too," said Luke. "Mullens told me that those two have actually had a civil discussion since the other night in the vineyard when Franny here beaned Max in the head."

"Really?" asked Owen. "I was sure that family feud would go on forever."

Luke shook his head. "Seems like this whole thing

brought it home to both of them that their rivalry has been silly, and that together, they might be able to create some amazing wines. I think they're going to be okay."

Alice felt a wave of relief at this news. "Then I'd like to propose a toast," she said, raising her bottle of water, and looking around the circle of the faces of her friends, her family. "To family. All families. But especially to this one."

"I'll drink to that!" said Owen.

Plastic bottles were clicked together and everyone took swigs of water.

"Let's all go flop on Alice and Luke's couch and watch a movie," said Franny.

"Great idea," said Owen.

"I'll pop the popcorn," said Alice, standing and stretching, following the group toward the French doors, which were standing open to the spring evening.

"Hey," said Luke softly from behind her.

Alice stopped and turned back.

"That was some honeymoon," he said, pulling her close.

"No kidding," said Alice with a smile, laying her head on his shoulder.

"Have I mentioned lately how glad I am that we got married?"

"No, I think it's been a while."

He pulled away a bit and looked at Alice's face, tucking a red curl behind her ear. "I'm really, really glad we got married," he said.

"So am I," said Alice. "And I always will be."

"I have a feeling, Mrs. Evans, that our love will age like a fine wine."

"Ooh, like an essencia?" said Alice, laughing. She kissed her husband. "Sweeter with the passing of the years."

"Ever sweeter," said Luke with a smile. He took her hand and they went inside to join their family.

AUTHOR'S NOTE

I'd love to hear your thoughts on my books, the story-lines, and anything else that you'd like to comment on —reader feedback is very important to me. My contact information, along with some other helpful links, is listed on the next page. If you'd like to be on my list of "folks to contact" with updates, release and sales notifications, etc.… just shoot me an email and let me know. Thanks for reading!

Also…

… if you're looking for more great reads, Summer Prescott Books publishes several popular series by outstanding Cozy Mystery authors.

CONTACT SUMMER PRESCOTT BOOKS PUBLISHING

Twitter: @summerprescott1

Bookbub: https://www.bookbub.com/authors/summer-prescott

Blog and Book Catalog: http://summerprescottbooks.com

Email: summer.prescott.cozies@gmail.com

YouTube: https://www.youtube.com/channel/UCngKNUkDdWuQ5k7-Vkfrp6A

And…be sure to check out the Summer Prescott Cozy Mysteries fan page and Summer Prescott Books Publishing Page on Facebook – let's be friends!

To download a free book, and sign up for our fun and exciting newsletter, which will give you opportunities to win prizes and swag, enter contests, and be the first to know about New Releases, click here: http://summerprescottbooks.com

Made in the USA
Monee, IL
18 February 2021